Ludwig
THE DOG WHO SNORED SYMPHONIES

by

Vip

Story by Robert Kraus

Windmill Books / Simon & Schuster
New York

For Rover the dog who snored symphonies
and
For the 7 K kids

Published by Windmill Books, Inc., and
Simon & Schuster, a Division of Gulf & Western Corporation
Simon & Schuster Building
1230 Avenue of the Americas
New York, New York 10020

WINDMILL BOOKS and colophon are trademarks of Windmill Books, Inc.,
registered in the U.S. Patent and Trademark Office.

Manufactured in the United States of America

10 9 8 7 6 5 4 3 2 1
Library of Congress Cataloging in Publication Data

Kraus, Robert,
Ludwig the dog who snored symphonies.

Reprint. Originally published: 1971.
Summary: A dog gains fame and fortune for himself
and his master by snoring nine symphonies.
[1. Dogs—Fiction.   2. Music—Fiction]   I. Vip,
1916-   II. Partch, Virgil Franklin, 1916-
III. Title.
PZ7.K868Lu 1981   [E]   81-7576
ISBN 0-671-43411-X   AACR2

Once upon a time, in the town of Dusseldorf, there lived a poor piccolo player named Emile. He played his piccolo on street corners, earning a meager living from the coins passersby tossed into his hat.

His faithful dog Ludwig was his only friend and kept him company as he played.

After playing all night, Emile and Ludwig would share a cup of coffee at an all-night café. "Don't worry, Ludwig," said Emile, "someday I shall finish my symphony and become rich and famous and we will have a wonderful life."

Then they would climb the winding stairs to the little attic studio they called home.

Emile would take off his shoes, tighten his ragged scarf and work on his unfinished symphony. Emile worked and worked until dawn, but when he finally put down his pencil he had written only one note and *that* was sour. Ludwig slept at Emile's feet and snored through it all.

The next night Emile worked on his symphony again with Ludwig sleeping and snoring at his feet. But again he could compose only one note and a sour one at that.

The next night it was more of the same thing. "At this rate it will take me two-hundred years to complete my symphony and I will be too old to enjoy it," moaned Emile, pulling his hair out in clumps. Ludwig snored on. "It's Ludwig's snoring! That's the trouble," he groaned. "Who can compose in the middle of all this snoring?"

Ludwig, not realizing all the commotion he was causing, snored on and on. Soon the only thing in Emile's mind was Ludwig's snoring. Suddenly Emile's face lit up. "Ludwig's snoring is beautiful!" he exclaimed. "Ludwig is snoring a symphony!"

So Emile grabbed his pencil and paper and wrote down the notes of the symphony Ludwig snored.

The next day he went to the maestro of the Symphony Orchestra to show him the symphony Ludwig had snored. Emile played part of it on his piccolo while the maestro hummed. Ludwig wagged his tail contentedly.

"Why this is magnificent!" said the maestro. "I will perform it with my Symphony Orchestra immediately. You are a genius!"

"Not I," said Emile. "Ludwig is the genius. He snored this symphony—I just wrote down the notes he snored."

"Extraordinary," said the maestro, shaking Ludwig's paw. "My congratulations to you, Ludwig. You are a genius!"

Ludwig wagged his tail happily.

Ludwig's symphony was performed by the
Dusseldorf Symphony Orchestra and was a great success.
Ludwig and Emile listened from a box. It was the first time
a dog had ever been allowed in Symphony Hall.

That night Emile and Ludwig went home tired but happy. They staggered through the after–theater traffic and narrowly missed being hit by two taxis and an omnibus.

They climbed the winding steps to the little attic studio. Once inside Ludwig fell asleep at Emile's feet and began to snore. Quickly Emile grabbed a pencil and paper. One half hour later Ludwig had snored his second symphony!

Symphony followed symphony (as Ludwig did a lot of snoring) and soon Ludwig had snored eight symphonies. Each one was performed by the Symphony Orchestra and was hailed as a masterpiece. Emile and Ludwig were able to afford a nicer garret and better food. They also saved a little money, and helped their less fortunate neighbors.

Dog owners from all over, hearing of Ludwig's success, copied down their dogs' snorings and brought them to the maestro of the Symphony Orchestra.

But they weren't symphonies. They were just dog snores.

The maestro's waiting room was crowded with masters and their dogs, waiting to show their dogs' compositions to the maestro. Each one was worse than the last. They weren't symphonies, they were just dog snores. "The difference between your dogs and Ludwig," said the maestro, "is talent."

"There is only one Ludwig and the world is eagerly awaiting the performance of his latest and greatest symphony—number nine. He is hard at work on it, or fast asleep, as the case may be. So please, all you dog owners, take your pets home and enjoy them for what they are—pets—not composers."

Emile and Ludwig *were* hard at work on Ludwig's next symphony. That was the trouble. Ludwig was hard at work when he should have been fast asleep. All the excitement of his sudden success had made him so nervous he couldn't sleep. And if he didn't sleep, he didn't snore. And no snore—no symphony.

Ludwig tried to bark his symphony, but it just came out dog barks.

He tried to growl his symphony, but it just came out dog growls.

He tried to tap out his symphony with his tail, but it just came out tail taps.

He tried to click out his symphony with his teeth, but it just came out teeth clicks.

Finally, Emile tried to write his symphony for him, but Emile could only write one note a night.

At last it was the morning of the day the unsnored symphony was to be performed—but no symphony.

Then it was the afternoon of the day Ludwig's unsnored symphony was to be performed—but no symphony.

Then it was the evening of the day Ludwig's unsnored symphony was to be performed—but still no symphony.

Ten minutes before curtain time!

"It's too late," moaned Emile. "We must now do the only honorable thing left to us. We must appear at Symphony Hall and tell the audience to go home."

So Emile and Ludwig staggered through the heavy theater traffic to Symphony Hall, narrowly missing being hit by several taxi cabs and an omnibus.

At last Emile and Ludwig staggered through the stage door and onto the stage to make the announcement that Ludwig's Ninth Symphony was not finished. They were both so tired that they fell asleep right on the stage in front of everybody and Ludwig began to snore!

He snored his Ninth Symphony in person in front of an enthusiastic audience. The musicians, as well as the audience, listened spellbound. Then the tympani joined in the rhythm, the violins picked up the melody and the wind instruments carried the tune until the great hall swelled with the sound of Ludwig's music.

When the symphony was over, Ludwig received a standing ovation, which woke him up. He caught the roses that were tossed to him and graciously acknowledged the applause doubly earned for the symphony he had composed as well as performed.

From that night on, Ludwig snored his symphonies in concert halls all over Europe. Critics everywhere hailed him as one of the great musical geniuses, be he man or dog, of this or any age.

The End